Murray, Laura K.
Wyoming

WITHDRAWN

CORE LIBRARY OF US STATES

Wyoming

BY LAURA K. MURRAY
CONTENT CONSULTANT
Brian Beadles, MA
Deputy State Preservation Officer
Wyoming State Historic Preservation Office

Core Library

An Imprint of Abdo Publishing
abdobooks.com

abdobooks.com

Published by Abdo Publishing, a division of ABDO, PO Box 398166, Minneapolis, Minnesota 55439. Copyright © 2023 by Abdo Consulting Group, Inc. International copyrights reserved in all countries. No part of this book may be reproduced in any form without written permission from the publisher. Core Library™ is a trademark and logo of Abdo Publishing.

Printed in the United States of America, North Mankato, Minnesota.
052022
092022

Cover Photo: Shutterstock Images
Interior Photos: Don Mammoser/Shutterstock Images, 4–5, 45; Red Line Editorial, 7 (Wyoming), 7 (USA); Travis J. Camp/Shutterstock Images, 10–11; Robert Larsen/Shutterstock Images, 13; VCG Wilson/Fine Art/Corbis Historical/Getty Images, 14; Filip Bjorkman/Shutterstock Images, 17 (flag); David Spates/Shutterstock Images, 17 (bird); Tom Reichner/Shutterstock Images, 17 (flower); Shutterstock Images, 17 (bison), 23, 32, 37; Ann Cantelow/Shutterstock Images, 17 (tree); Dmitry Kovba/Shutterstock Images, 20–21, 43; Scott Canning/Shutterstock Images, 26; Russell Lee/ US National Archives/Smith Collection/Gado/Archive Photos/Getty Images, 28–29; Steve Boice/Shutterstock Images, 33; Chris Elise/Icon Sportswire/AP Images, 34–35; Vicki L. Miller/Shutterstock Images, 40

Editor: Angela Lim
Series Designer: Joshua Olson

Library of Congress Control Number: 2021951569

Publisher's Cataloging-in-Publication Data

Names: Murray, Laura K., author.
Title: Wyoming / by Laura K. Murray
Description: Minneapolis, Minnesota : Abdo Publishing, 2023 | Series: Core library of US states | Includes online resources and index.
Identifiers: ISBN 9781532197932 (lib. bdg.) | ISBN 9781098270698 (ebook)
Subjects: LCSH: U.S. states--Juvenile literature. | Western States (U.S.)--Juvenile literature. | Wyoming--History--Juvenile literature. | Physical geography--United States--Juvenile literature.
Classification: DDC 978.7--dc23

Population demographics broken down by race and ethnicity come from the 2019 census estimate. Population totals come from the 2020 census.

CONTENTS

CHAPTER ONE
The Equality State 4

CHAPTER TWO
History of Wyoming 10

CHAPTER THREE
Geography and Climate 20

CHAPTER FOUR
Resources and Economy 28

CHAPTER FIVE
People and Places 34

Important Dates 42

Stop and Think 44

Glossary 46

Online Resources 47

Learn More 47

Index 48

About the Author 48

CHAPTER ONE

THE EQUALITY STATE

Clouds of steam billow over the Grand Prismatic Spring in Yellowstone National Park. Visitors cross the boardwalk to see the hot spring ringed with hues of bright blue, green, yellow, orange, and red. Its vivid colors are formed by different kinds of heat-loving bacteria. The center of the pool reaches temperatures of 189 degrees Fahrenheit (87°C).

Yellowstone National Park is located in the northwestern corner of Wyoming and stretches

The Grand Prismatic Spring is the third-largest spring in the world.

into Montana and Idaho. In 1872 Yellowstone became the first national park in US history. Visitors from all over the world come to take in the views.

PERSPECTIVES

THE WONDER OF YELLOWSTONE

Nature writer John Muir fought to protect wilderness areas and create national parks. In 1898 Muir wrote about Yellowstone:

> *Beside the treasures common to most mountain regions that are wild and blessed with a kind climate, the park is full of exciting wonders. The wildest geysers in the world, in bright, triumphant bands, are dancing and singing in it amid thousands of boiling springs, beautiful and awful, their basins [displayed] in gorgeous colors like gigantic flowers.*

ABOUT WYOMING

Wyoming is part of the western region of the United States. It borders six US states. Montana borders it to the north and northwest. Idaho lies to its west, and Utah sits to its southwest. Colorado is located to its south. Nebraska and South Dakota make up Wyoming's eastern border.

MAP OF
WYOMING

Wyoming is known for its outdoor spaces. How does this map help you understand what the state has to offer?

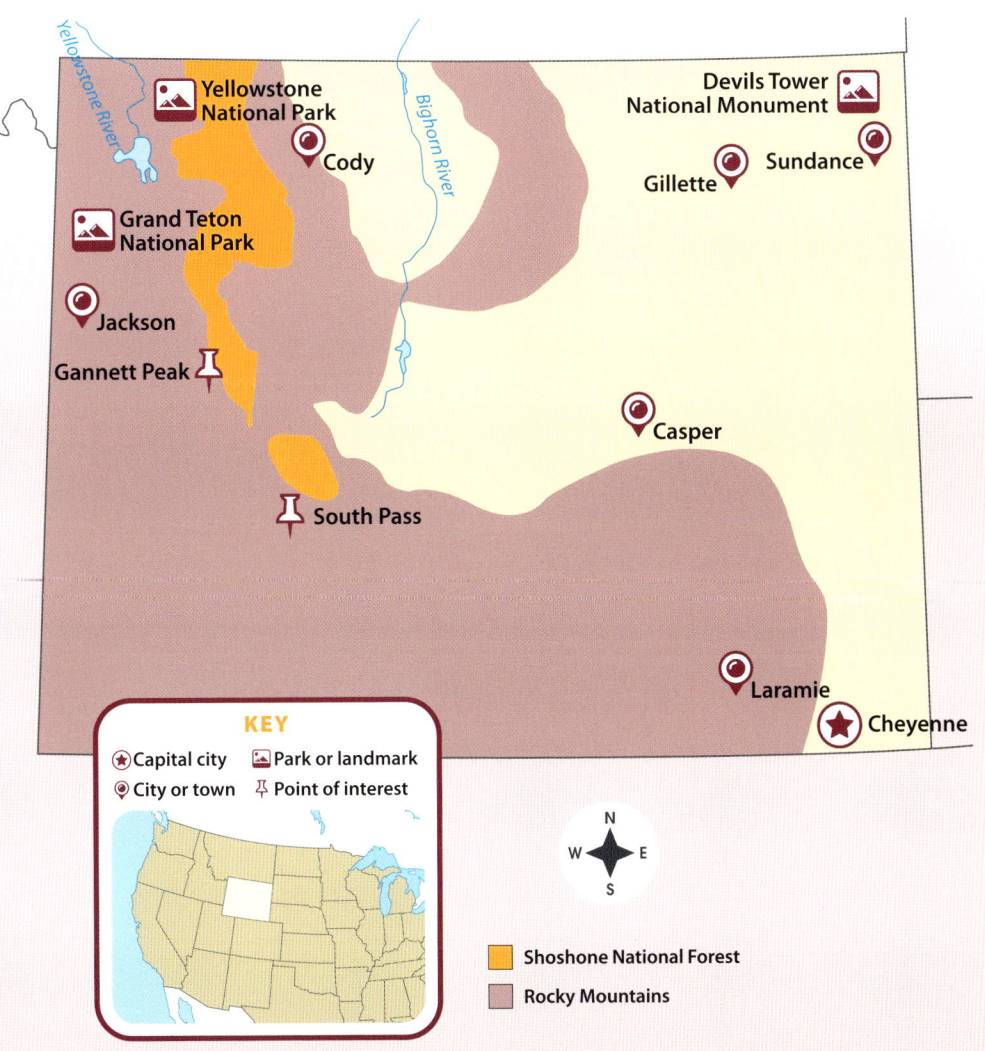

> ## BUCKING HORSE AND RIDER
> The Bucking Horse and Rider (BH&R) logo has been associated with Wyoming since at least 1918. During World War I (1914–1918), the emblem was worn by Wyoming National Guard members stationed in France and Germany. In 1936 the BH&R appeared on the state's license plates. Today the image is a registered trademark of the state as well as a symbol of pride for Wyomingites.

Wyoming is known as the Equality State. The nickname comes from the state's history of women's rights. In 1869 the Wyoming Territory gave women the right to vote. When Wyoming became a US state in 1890, it was the first state to allow women to vote. The US government did not give women this right until 1920.

Cheyenne is Wyoming's capital city and most populated city. Other major towns include Casper, Laramie, and Gillette. Cody and Jackson are known for their wild landscapes. Throughout the state, there are natural wonders to explore.

STRAIGHT TO THE SOURCE

On March 1, 1872, US president Ulysses S. Grant signed an act into law to establish Yellowstone as the country's first national park. The act reads:

> *Be it enacted by the Senate and House of Representatives of the United States of America in Congress assembled, That the tract of land in the Territories of Montana and Wyoming, lying near the headwaters of the Yellowstone River [and the described borders] is hereby reserved and withdrawn from settlement, occupancy, or sale under the laws of the United States, and dedicated and set apart as a public park or pleasuring-ground for the benefit and enjoyment of the people; and all persons who shall locate or settle upon or occupy the same, or any part thereof, except as hereinafter provided, shall be considered trespassers and removed therefrom.*
>
> Source: "Transcript of Act Establishing Yellowstone National Park (1872)." *Our Documents*, n.d., ourdocuments.gov. Accessed 30 July 2021.

WHAT'S THE BIG IDEA?

Read the act carefully. What is its main idea? How is the main idea supported by details? Name two or three of the supporting details.

CHAPTER TWO

HISTORY OF WYOMING

People have lived in Wyoming for at least 12,000 years. By the 1800s many American Indian nations were established in the Wyoming area. They included the Arapaho, Cheyenne, Lakota, Shoshone, Ute, and many others.

In 1803 the US government bought a large area of land from France. It was called the Louisiana Purchase. The land included much of present-day Wyoming. Meriwether Lewis and William Clark led an exploration group into

The Arapaho and the Cheyenne are just some of the many nations with cultural ties to the Medicine Wheel in the Bighorn Mountains.

the new region. They reached the Pacific Ocean before turning around. John Colter was part of the expedition. He remained in the western region with fur traders while the rest of the group returned east. In 1807 he became the first US explorer to enter the Wyoming region. Colter documented hydrothermal features that may be located in what is now Yellowstone National Park.

Explorers brought back news of large beaver populations in the western lands. Soon many US fur traders moved to the Wyoming area. They continued exploring the region, locating the South Pass. This plateau was an important passage through the Rocky Mountains. Historic trails including the Oregon Trail crossed through the South Pass. They allowed American settlers to move farther west.

The arrival of settlers changed the lives of the American Indians. The settlers carried diseases that killed many American Indians. Settlers also brought guns, which affected trade and warfare. American Indian

More than 350,000 white settlers traveled through the South Pass between 1841 and 1869.

nations that traded for bigger and better guns became more powerful than those that did not.

EXPANSION AND CONFLICT

At the end of the Mexican-American War (1846–1848), the Mexican and US governments agreed to the Treaty of Guadalupe Hidalgo. This added land to the United States, including southwestern Wyoming. The Homestead Act of 1862 opened large areas of land for settlement. US settlers could claim 160 acres (65 ha) of

The Dale Creek Bridge in Buford, Wyoming, was first built in 1868 as part of the Union Pacific Railroad. It was later replaced and eventually taken apart.

land for a small fee. They would own the property after living on the land for five years.

The Union Pacific Railroad encouraged many to settle in Wyoming. This was part of the first railroad to span the United States. It reached Cheyenne in 1867. As homesteaders claimed more land in the 1870s, the cattle industry boomed.

American settlers pushed American Indians out of their homelands in Wyoming and other areas. This caused many conflicts. For example the US Army killed 150 Cheyenne people in the Colorado Territory. In response a Cheyenne man named Roman Nose (Woquini) and an Oglala Lakota man named Red Cloud

(Mahpiua Luta) attacked US troops outside of Fort Caspar. Red Cloud led other attacks against US forts to protect American Indian land. These attacks are known as Red Cloud's War (1866–1868). Ultimately Red Cloud was able to drive out the US Army. After signing the Treaty of Fort Laramie in 1868, US troops left the area.

STATEHOOD AND GOVERNMENT

More settlers entered the region. The US Congress created the Wyoming Territory in 1868. In 1870 Esther Hobart Morris began serving in the South Pass city government. She was the first

JOHNSON COUNTY WAR

Wyoming's cattle industry boomed from the late 1860s to the 1880s. But cattle prices suddenly dropped in the early 1880s. Drought and a harsh winter caused the industry to decline further. Conflicts arose between ranchers and business owners as they competed for land and livestock. In April 1892 these conflicts turned deadly. US soldiers came to end the conflict. But violence continued for years afterward. The events became known as the Johnson County War.

woman in the United States to hold judicial public office. On July 10, 1890, Wyoming was admitted into the Union as the forty-fourth state. In 1925 Wyoming's Nellie Tayloe Ross became the first female governor in the United States. She later became the first female mint director of the US Mint in 1933. This government division produces all US coins.

Wyoming sent more than 30,000 soldiers to fight in World War II (1939–1945). The United States fought Japan, Germany, and other countries. Because of Japan's role in the war, the US government distrusted Japanese Americans. Many Japanese Americans were forced to live in concentration camps. The Heart Mountain Relocation Center was one of these concentration camps. It was in northwestern Wyoming. The center closed in 1945.

Today the Wyoming government has a legislative, executive, and judicial branch. These branches respectively create, enforce, and interpret laws.

WYOMING
QUICK FACTS

Take a look at Wyoming's nickname and motto. How do they represent the state's history?

Abbreviation: WY
Nickname: The Equality State
Motto: Equal rights
Date of statehood: July 10, 1890
Capital: Cheyenne
Population: 576,851
Area: 97,813 square miles (253,335 sq km)

STATE SYMBOLS

State bird
Western meadowlark

State mammal
American bison

State flower
Indian paintbrush

State tree
Plains cottonwood

The Wind River Reservation in Wyoming is home to two federally recognized American Indian nations. They are the Northern Arapaho Tribe and the Eastern Shoshone Tribe. Each nation has its own leadership that is separate from the state government. Many other American Indian nations have ties to Wyoming but were historically forced from the region.

PERSPECTIVES

THE WYOMING 14

In October 1969 the University of Wyoming's head football coach kicked 14 Black players off the team. The players had asked to wear black armbands during a game to protest racism. The players became known as the Wyoming 14. In 2019 the school invited them back for a public apology. People cheered as the players walked onto the field. "I had to throw up the peace sign to show [the crowd] we love them as much as they love us," said player Joe Williams. "I wanted to honor them for listening to our story. It felt so great, like I went back to see old friends."

STRAIGHT TO THE SOURCE

Nellie Tayloe Ross was the fourteenth governor of Wyoming. In 1927 she wrote a magazine article about her time as governor:

> *Though I did not say so at the time, I could never escape the feeling that more sustained and diligent attention would be expected of me than would have been expected of a man. Because a woman in the governorship was an experiment, her every act . . . was under constant public scrutiny, and I felt that every mistake would be used to challenge the qualifications of women to hold high office.*
>
> Source: Nellie Tayloe Ross. "The Governor Lady: The Dramatic Story of a Wife Who Put Aside Her Grief to Carry On Her Husband's Unfinished Work." *Good Housekeeping*, Oct. 1927, digitalcollections.uwyo.edu. Accessed 6 Aug. 2021.

CONSIDER YOUR AUDIENCE

Review this passage closely. Consider how you would adapt it for a different audience, such as your parents, your principal, or younger friends. Write a blog post conveying this same information to the new audience. How does your blog post differ from the original text?

CHAPTER THREE

GEOGRAPHY AND CLIMATE

The Rocky Mountains cover western Wyoming. These mountains give the state a high average elevation of 6,700 feet (2,040 m). Colorado is the only US state with a higher average. The Rockies are made up of many mountain ranges including the Tetons, the Bighorn Mountains, and the Wind River Range. The Rocky Mountains form a continental divide. This is when elevation causes rivers to flow in different directions. Rivers on one side of the divide travel west

The Yellowstone Caldera helps form Old Faithful and other geysers in Yellowstone National Park.

YELLOWSTONE VOLCANO OBSERVATORY

Scientists closely study earthquake and volcanic activity at Yellowstone. The Yellowstone Volcano Observatory was formed in 2001. It is made up of scientists from state and federal agencies. The scientists track Yellowstone's earthquakes, ground movement, and volcanic activity. They do not predict a large eruption in the near future.

toward the Pacific Ocean. On the other side, rivers flow eastward into the Atlantic Ocean.

Yellowstone is also found in the western region. Much of the park sits on top of a massive volcanic system called the Yellowstone Caldera. A caldera is a large crater that forms when a volcano erupts. Several major eruptions have occurred in the Yellowstone region. The eruption that formed the Yellowstone Caldera happened 640,000 years ago.

The Great Plains cover eastern Wyoming. They include grasslands and prairies. The Black Hills are also

Grand Teton National Park receives more than 170 inches (430 cm) of snow each year.

located within this region. They stretch from South Dakota into northeastern Wyoming. The rocky Black Hills rise up from the surrounding plains.

CLIMATE

Wyoming's different elevations and land features affect the climate. High elevations tend to be cooler than low elevations. Summer temperatures can reach 95 degrees

Fahrenheit (35°C). Winter temperatures may drop below 5 degrees Fahrenheit (−15°C).

Western Wyoming receives more rain and snow than the eastern region. The Bighorn Basin in northern Wyoming is the driest part of the state. It gets less than 8 inches (20 cm) of rain each year on average. It also receives 15 to 20 inches (38–51 cm) of snow annually. Mountain regions receive much more snow. Some areas in Yellowstone average more than 200 inches (510 cm) per year.

Snowmelt is an important water resource for Wyoming. It is used for watering crops, creating electricity, and other everyday purposes. But climate change is causing snow to melt earlier than it did in previous decades. This change in weather patterns affects wildlife and people's lifestyles.

Wyoming experiences extreme weather. Droughts and blizzards affect the state. Hailstorms can damage crops and property. Melting snow and thunderstorms can cause flooding. In recent years, summers have become hotter and drier. This has caused wildfires to become larger and more frequent.

WILDLIFE

The US government owns approximately 48 percent of Wyoming's land. This includes the state's national forests, national parks, and other protected wilderness areas. The Shoshone National Forest is in northwestern

PERSPECTIVES

RETURN OF THE WOLVES

In the early 1900s, farmers and ranchers killed many gray wolves to protect their livestock. The wolves became endangered. In 1995 wildlife officials began to release gray wolves into Yellowstone. Many ranchers were unhappy with this decision. But the efforts of the wildlife officials paid off. In 2017 the wolves were removed from the endangered species list in Wyoming. The wolves helped balance the numbers of other animals in Yellowstone. Mike Phillips was one of the scientists who worked to restore wolves to the region. He said, "We recognized the need for wolf recovery to go forward even though it was difficult."

Bison have thick winter coats that allow them to withstand cold temperatures and heavy snow.

Wyoming. It became the country's first national forest in 1891. Gannett Peak lies within the forest. It is Wyoming's highest point, rising 13,785 feet (4,202 m) above sea level.

Mammals such as bison, grizzly bears, black bears, moose, and pronghorn antelope can all be found in Yellowstone. The state is home to many birds, including prairie falcons and western meadowlarks. The horned toad is the state reptile. Despite its name, it is actually a lizard. It is known for its pointy spines that look like horns. Other reptiles include the great basin skink and prairie rattlesnake. The state amphibian is the blotched tiger salamander. It lives in moist places including rodent burrows.

Wyoming is known for its sagebrush landscapes. Native plants include mule-ears and bitterroot. Colorful wildflowers such as Indian paintbrush and harebell grow. The lodgepole pine, ponderosa pine, and plains cottonwood are common trees in Wyoming.

EXPLORE ONLINE

Chapter Three discusses wildlife at Yellowstone National Park. The video at the website below goes into more depth on this topic. Compare the information on the website with the information in the chapter. Does the website answer any questions you had about Yellowstone?

YELLOWSTONE, THE FIRST NATIONAL PARK
abdocorelibrary.com/wyoming

CHAPTER FOUR

RESOURCES AND ECONOMY

Wyoming's main industry is mining. The state has been the top coal producer in the United States since 1986. It produces more than 39 percent of the country's coal supply. In 2020 the state produced 218 million tons (198 million metric tons) of coal. Coal production has declined as the state has begun using other fossil fuels.

Wyoming is a top-ten producer of crude oil and natural gas in the United States.

This 1946 photograph shows Wyoming women sorting coal from other materials.

Most of Wyoming's natural gas comes from the southwestern part of the state. The state's first oil well was drilled in 1884. In 2020 Wyoming produced more than 89 million barrels of crude oil. Wyoming also has large amounts of trona. This mineral is used to make glass, baking soda, and other products.

In 2020 renewable energy made up approximately 15 percent of Wyoming's total electricity.

PERSPECTIVES

FROM COAL COUNTRY TO WIND COUNTRY?

In recent years, people in Wyoming have disagreed about the future of resources in their state. Some people want to stay focused on mining coal. Others say that the state should develop renewable energy instead. "Coal is on the way out," said Connie Wilbert in 2021. She was the director of the Wyoming chapter of the Sierra Club, an environmental organization. "The sooner our elected leadership acknowledges that and starts looking for things the state can do to actually help us through the transition, the better."

Most renewable energy came from wind. The mountains drive winds across the state's open plains. This makes the state a good location for wind power. Wyoming's use of wind energy more than doubled between 2009 and 2020. Hydroelectric power is the state's next largest source of renewable energy.

TOURISM AND AGRICULTURE

Tourism is the second-largest industry in Wyoming. In 2019 visitors spent $3.9 billion in the state. The tourism industry supported more than 32,480 jobs. Teton County is the most visited county. It is home to much of

FOSSIL FINDS

Wyoming is a popular tourist destination for fossil hunters. The state's public lands are home to some of the oldest fossils in the world. Cities such as Kemmerer invite visitors to dig for fossils. The allosaurus is a dinosaur that lived approximately 145 million years ago. An allosaurus skeleton is on display at the University of Wyoming in Laramie. Scientists found the skeleton in northern Wyoming's Bighorn County in 1991. They nicknamed the skeleton "Big Al."

Jackson Hole Mountain Resort is a popular destination for skiers.

Yellowstone National Park and Grand Teton National Park. Teton County is also home to Jackson Hole, a valley that is popular for skiing and hiking.

Agriculture is an important part of Wyoming's economy. The state's largest agricultural product is beef cattle. Wyoming is the country's second-leading producer of sheep. The state also produces hay that is used for animal feed. Other crops include sugar beets, dry beans, and barley.

Wyoming was the US leader in wool production in 2017.

CHAPTER FIVE

PEOPLE AND PLACES

With a population of 576,851, Wyoming is the least populated state. White people who are not Hispanic or Latino make up 84 percent of the population. Hispanic or Latino people total 10 percent. American Indians are 2.7 percent of the population. Black and Asian people each make up approximately 1 percent of the state's population.

Several well-known people hail from Wyoming. Children's book author Patricia

Bull riding is part of the rodeo competition in Cheyenne's Frontier Days celebration.

35

MacLachlan was born in 1938 in Cheyenne. She wrote the children's book *Sarah, Plain and Tall*. Jackson Pollock was born in Cody in 1912. He is a famous artist known for his paintings that look like drips and splashes. Dick Cheney served as vice president of the United States under George W. Bush from 2001 to 2009. He grew up in Casper. In 2016 Cheney's daughter Liz was elected as a US representative for Wyoming.

PERSPECTIVES
DEVILS TOWER

The Devils Tower rock formation is a sacred site for many American Indians. The Lakota call the formation *Mato Tipila*, which means "Bear Rock." Mistranslations led to the name Devils Tower. For many years American Indian nations have tried to get the tower renamed. Chief Arvol Looking Horse is the spiritual leader of the Great Sioux Nation. "It hurts us to think about such a beautiful, sacred place called Devils Tower," he said in 2016. "[It is] a sacred site that's like a church, a place of worship."

PLACES TO VISIT

Many people visit Wyoming to enjoy the outdoors and take in the beautiful views at

Devils Tower rises above the surrounding prairies.

its national and state parks. Grand Teton National Park is in northwestern Wyoming near Yellowstone. The park includes the Teton Range, as well as mountain lakes, meadows, and forests. Another well-known destination is Devils Tower in the Black Hills. The 867-foot (264-m) butte became the first US national monument in 1906.

Visitors to Wyoming enjoy all kinds of outdoor activities. They camp, hike, and ride horses. Nearly 550 miles (885 km) of the Continental Divide Trail are located in Wyoming. People can fish or float down a river in inner tubes. Thrill-seeking visitors go rock climbing and zip-lining. Snowshoeing and skiing are

OUTLAW HISTORY

Famous outlaws made their marks in Wyoming throughout the 1800s. For example Butch Cassidy and the Sundance Kid's cabin hideout was located near Kaycee, Wyoming. The cabin stood near the Bighorn Mountains, in a region nicknamed "Hole-in-the-Wall." It was later moved to Cody. Today this site and many others are tourist attractions. Cody celebrates its outlaw history at Old Trail Town. Visitors can experience an old-fashioned western town with saloons and blacksmith shops.

popular winter options. Some people even go ice climbing, which involves climbing frozen waterfalls.

Wyoming also has its share of historical sites. The Fort Laramie National Historic Site offers tours of the fort's restored buildings from the 1800s. Sites along the Oregon Trail include the Independence Rock Historic Site. Many American settlers carved their names into the rock as they made their journey west. The Medicine Mountain National Historic Landmark is in Bighorn National Forest. The area includes a circle of stones known as the Medicine Wheel. Medicine Mountain has connections to American Indian nations such as the Crow and the Shoshone. The mountain has been a site for trade and important American Indian ceremonies for approximately 7,000 years.

GETTING TOGETHER

Visitors can experience Wyoming's history and culture through celebrations and festivals. Rodeo is Wyoming's state sport. Rodeo athletes show off their skills in handling horses and livestock. Events include bull riding, barrel racing, and roping. Cheyenne's Frontier Days event is the world's largest outdoor rodeo. The annual summer event includes wild-horse racing, cooking contests, and an art show.

American Indian nations including the Shoshone and the Arapaho hold cultural celebrations called powwows. The Eastern Shoshone Indian Days Powwow is the largest powwow in the state. It takes place on the Wind River Indian Reservation. Visitors can learn about

Shoshone culture. The powwow includes traditional food, dances, and art.

Skiing, snowboarding, and other sports competitions take place in the winter. Sundance holds skijoring races. Skijoring racers ski while being tethered to a horse. Whether attending a local rodeo, enjoying natural wonders, or visiting a historical site, visitors to Wyoming have an experience like no other.

FURTHER EVIDENCE

Chapter Five discusses things to do and see in Wyoming. Identify one of the author's main points. What evidence does the author provide to support this point? The website at the link below also discusses the topic. Find a quote on this website that supports the author's main point. Does it offer a new piece of evidence?

WYOMING'S STATE PARKS ARE ROAD TRIP DESTINATIONS

abdocorelibrary.com/wyoming

American Indian performers wore traditional clothing during a 2015 powwow in Cheyenne.

IMPORTANT DATES

640,000 years ago
A massive volcanic eruption forms the Yellowstone Caldera.

12,000 years ago
Early peoples live in what is now Wyoming.

1807
John Colter becomes the first American explorer to enter the Wyoming region.

1866
Red Cloud's War begins. The Lakota leader organizes attacks on US forts to protect American Indian land.

1868
The US Congress creates the Wyoming Territory.

1869
The Wyoming Territory gives women the right to vote and hold public office.

1872
Yellowstone National Park becomes the first national park in US history.

1890
Wyoming becomes the forty-fourth US state on July 10.

1925
Nellie Tayloe Ross begins service as the governor of Wyoming, becoming the first female governor in the United States.

2001
The Yellowstone Volcano Observatory is formed to study earthquakes and volcanic activity in the area.

STOP AND THINK

Dig Deeper
After reading this book, what questions do you still have about Nellie Tayloe Ross or other women in Wyoming's history? With an adult's help, find a few reliable sources that can help you answer your questions. Write a paragraph about what you learned.

Why Do I Care?
Chapter Four discusses different views on fossil fuels and renewable energy. Do you think it is important for states to use renewable energy? Why or why not? How do energy sources affect your life? How might your life be different if an energy source is used up?

You Are There
Chapter One discusses Yellowstone National Park. Imagine you are camping in Yellowstone. Write a letter home telling your friends about your experience. What types of volcanic or hydrothermal features do you see? What wildlife do you see? Be sure to add plenty of detail to your notes.

Another View

This book talks about Red Cloud's War. As you know, every source is different. Ask a librarian or another adult to help you find another source about this event. Write a short essay comparing and contrasting the new source's point of view with that of this book's author. What is the point of view of each author? How are they similar and why? How are they different and why?

GLOSSARY

butte
an isolated hill or mountain with steep sides and a flat top

concentration camp
a place where an army or military holds a large number of people, especially those of a specific culture or religion

fossil fuel
a natural fuel such as oil, gas, or coal formed by fossilized plants and animals

geyser
a spring that occasionally erupts in bursts of hot water and steam

homestead
land given by the US government that becomes personal property after a person takes care of it for some years

hydroelectric
electricity generated by flowing water

hydrothermal
relating to hot water, especially under the surface of the earth

plateau
high, flat land

sacred
having religious importance

ONLINE RESOURCES

To learn more about Wyoming, visit our free resource websites below.

Visit **abdocorelibrary.com** or scan this QR code for free Common Core resources for teachers and students, including vetted activities, multimedia, and booklinks, for deeper subject comprehension.

Visit a**bdobooklinks.com** or scan this QR code for free additional online weblinks for further learning. These links are routinely monitored and updated to provide the most current information available.

LEARN MORE

Isabella, Jude. *Bringing Back the Wolves: How a Predator Restored an Ecosystem*. Kids Can, 2020.

London, Martha. *Fact and Fiction of the Wild West*. Abdo, 2022.

INDEX

American Indians, 11–12, 14–15, 18, 35, 36, 39–41

Cheyenne, 7, 8, 14, 17, 36, 39
climate, 6, 23–25
Cody, 7, 8, 36, 38
Colter, John, 12

Devils Tower National Monument, 7, 36, 37

energy, 30–31

forests, 7, 25–26, 37–38

Grand Teton National Park, 7, 33, 37
Great Plains, 22–23

homesteads, 13–14

Jackson, 7, 8

Medicine Wheel, 38–39
mining, 29–30

Oregon Trail, 12, 38

Red Cloud, 14–15
rivers, 7, 9, 21–22, 37
Rocky Mountains, 7, 12, 21

rodeos, 39–41
Ross, Nellie Tayloe, 16, 19

skiing, 33, 37, 41
South Pass, 7, 12, 15

volcanoes, 22

wolves, 25
women's rights, 8, 15–16, 19

Yellowstone National Park, 5–6, 7, 9, 12, 22, 24–27, 33, 37

About the Author

Laura K. Murray has written more than 90 nonfiction books on subjects ranging from music and pop culture to history and science. She loves to visit new places in person and through books!